Nicoll Road Nursery

For Eddie, Lewis, Hayley, Jake and Kate – A.H.
For Linda Lyall – M.M.

First published in Great Britain in 1987
This revised edition published in 2007
by Piccadilly Press Ltd,
5 Castle Road, London NW1 8PR
www.piccadillypress.co.uk

Designed by Simon Davis
Printed and bound in China by WKT
Colour reproduction by Dot Gradations

ISBN: 978 1 85340 905 9 (hardback)
ISBN: 978 1 85340 897 7 (paperback)

3 5 7 9 10 8 6 4 2

A catalogue record of this book is
available from the British Library

It's Not Fair!

By Anita Harper
Illustrated by Mary McQuillan

Piccadilly Press ● London

When Mum and Dad brought my baby brother home, everyone fussed over him.

It wasn't fair!

"What about me?"
"You're a big girl now," my mum said.

I'm not **THAT** big.

People are always doing things for HIM.
I have to do things for myself.

It's not fair!

If he makes a mess, it's all right.

If I make a mess, I get into trouble.
That's not fair!

When we go out, I have to walk.

But my baby brother can ride.

It makes me MAD!

When the babysitter is here,
and my brother screams,
she tries to find out what's wrong.

When I scream
she tells me to be quiet.

It's not fair!

Now my brother's getting bigger. The other day, we went for a walk in the rain. He wanted to walk, but my mum wouldn't let him.

He didn't think
that was fair!

And when we go to the park
he wants to slide down the hill,
but HE isn't big enough.

He doesn't think
THAT'S fair either!

When I go to playgroup,
my brother wants to go too,
but he can't.

He doesn't think **THAT'S** fair at all.

Now, when my friends come over, my brother wants to play with us,

but he's too small.

He lets us know he doesn't think that's fair.

Sometimes I'm allowed to stay up late,
but my brother has to go to bed.

He screams and screams, because
it's not fair!

My brother has started to talk now.
Today I'm going to a party
and he can't go.

Do you know what he said?

"It's not fair!"